DATE DUE   77-100 2974

JAN 24 1983

I don't care

I don't care

By Marjorie Weinman Sharmat

Pictures by Lillian Hoban

MACMILLAN PUBLISHING CO., INC.
New York

COLLIER MACMILLAN PUBLISHERS
London

Macmillan Publishing Co., Inc.
866 Third Avenue, New York, N. Y. 10022
Collier Macmillan Canada, Ltd.

Printed in the United States of America

10 9 8 7 6 5 4 3 2 1

Library of Congress Cataloging in Publication Data

Sharmat, Marjorie Weinman.
    I don't care.
Summary: A young boy discovers that denying his
grief doesn't make it disappear.
[1. Grief—Fiction]   I. Hoban, Lillian.   II. Title.
PZ7.S5299Id   [E]   76–48251   ISBN 0–02–782290–7

For Lil and Hy Silver

Jonathan had a balloon.
It was blue and round
and had a smiling face on it.
Jonathan liked to let his balloon
rise slowly
till its long string was used up.
He liked to watch it
go higher and higher
and look smaller and smaller.
He liked to pull the string back
and watch the balloon get bigger and bigger
as it came closer.

Once as Jonathan was holding his balloon
by the end of its string,
it slipped from his fingers.
"Oh!"
Jonathan saw the balloon
go higher and higher
and get smaller and smaller.

"Come back!" he yelled.

But the balloon was gone.

Jonathan sat down.
He sat for a long time.

Then he went into the house.
"My dumb balloon blew away,"
he said to his father.

"I will get you a new balloon,
   just like the old one,"
   his father said.

"No," said Jonathan.
"A new one is never like an old one
   because you have the old one first."

Jonathan went back outside.
"I don't care. It was just a dumb balloon,"
he said to himself.
"I don't care if it blew away."

"I don't care!" Jonathan yelled to the sky.

"I don't care!"

Jonathan went to Brandon's house.

"My dumb, stupid balloon blew away," he said.

"I never heard of a dumb, stupid balloon,"
said Brandon.

"I'm not even going to think
about that balloon any more,"
said Jonathan.

Jonathan went home. He sat on his front steps.
"Dumb balloon," he said loudly.
"I'm not thinking about you."

At lunch Jonathan said, "I'm not thinking about
my balloon any more. I don't care if it's gone."
"That's good," said Jonathan's father.

An hour later Jonathan said to his mother,
"I'm still not thinking about my balloon."
"I'm glad to hear that," said Jonathan's mother.

Jonathan spent the afternoon playing with his toys.
"Who wants a balloon?" he said.

But when suppertime came,
Jonathan didn't feel like eating.
He went outside and looked up at the sky.
He looked and looked.
Then he yelled, "It's gone! It's gone!
My balloon is gone!"

Suddenly Jonathan's eyes filled with tears.
He blinked them back.
He blinked again, and again.

Then Jonathan opened his mouth.
"WAAAAAAAAAAAH!"

Jonathan started to cry.
He cried and cried.

He ran around the block and cried.
He ran into his house and cried.

He ran past his mother and father
and up to his room and cried.

He put away his toys
and cried.
Then he just sat and cried.

After a while Jonathan came downstairs
to his mother and father.
"I'm done," he said.

His parents hugged him.
And they all sat down to supper.